W9-AUD-895

Martha Alexander

I'll Protect You from the Jungle Beasts

Charlesbridge

Published by Charlesbridge
85 Main Street
Watertown, MA 02472
(617) 926-0329
www.charlesbridge.com

Library of Congress Cataloging-in-Publication Data
Alexander, Martha G.
I'll protect you from the jungle beasts / Martha Alexander.
p. cm.
Summary: A little boy explains how he will protect his teddy bear from the beasts
in the forest, then he becomes lost and the teddy bear's stuffing takes over.
ISBN-13: 978-1-57091-677-9; ISBN-10: 1-57091-677-2 (reinforced for library use)
[1. Teddy bears—Fiction. 2. Toys—Fiction. 3. Imagination—Fiction.]
I. Title: I will protect you from the jungle beasts. II. Title.
PZ7.A3777Il   2006
[E]—dc22
2005019618

Printed in China
(hc) 10 9 8 7 6 5 4 3 2 1

Illustrations recolorized with watercolor and colored pencil
on the pages of a first-edition printing of the original book
Display type and text type set in Roger and New Aster
Color separations by Chroma Graphics, Singapore
Printed and bound by Jade Productions
Production supervision by Brian G. Walker
Designed by Diane M. Earley

Oh, yes, Teddy, there are lions and tigers and elephants in this forest—big ones. But don't worry. I'll protect you from the jungle beasts.

Yes, they *are* fierce, but I won't let them
hurt you. Do snakes eat teddy bears?
Well, not if they have someone to protect them.

You really mustn't worry. That was
a very old lion. I could tell by his roar.

I'm sure he's toothless and too tired
to even run. And I can run like the wind.

Or I could hit him between the eyes
with my slingshot.

Don't be frightened, Teddy!

HA!HA! HA!

HEEE E E E

HAHAHA

HA HA HAHA HA HA HAHAHAHA

I think that was a hyena. They *do* have spooky laughs. No, I really don't think they eat teddy bears.

Boys? Oh, I'm not sure. There's a big club.
I can smash him to bits if he comes near us.

No, I'm not frightened.

Well, I *thought* this was the path home.
Do you see any lights anywhere?

Lost?
Well, I don't know. I wish I'd brought
my compass with me.

You have what—a built-in home finder?
That must be something only teddy bears
have. A special kind of stuffing? Oh.

GRRRR
R
RRRR
RRRRRRRRR
GRRRRRRRR

Yes, that was very close.
It must be enormous.

Shaking? Me? I must be getting
a fever or something.

If I get sick it might be hard to clobber
a big, fierce animal. I always feel weak
when I have a fever.

Perspiration? That must be
from the fever I'm getting.

Boy, I wish I were filled with stuffing.
Then I wouldn't have this fever.

My knees are a little weak.
Lean on you? Oh, good.

You *are* strong. Your stuffing?
I wish *I* had special stuffing.

Oh, Teddy, I feel better already.
My fever seems to be going away, too.

Look! There's our house!

It's nice to be in our own bed again . . .

. . . isn't it?

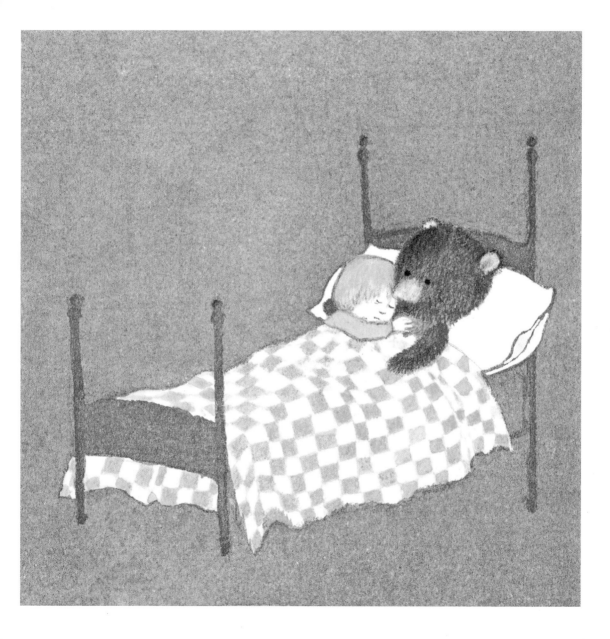

Good morning, Teddy!
How's your stuffing?